COTTON BREAD

16 Bedtime Stories for Kids Ages 4-8

Short Bedtime Stories, and Fairy Tales Collections for Children – Illustrated

First edition

This book was professionally typeset on Reedsy.
Find out more at reedsy.com

Contents

About the Author

Cotton Bread has a mind full of wonderful and creative ideas. She loves to create lively, unique, warm, and loving educational stories for children.

When we were kids, we all dreamed of a colorful place with lots of delicious food and fun things to do. These beautiful dreams made life better and more exciting.

Cotton Bread is an author who creates simple and fun stories. Children can learn how to love and care for their parents, friends, and pets through these magical and exciting tales. Without dreams and imagination, life can feel empty.

It is hoped that everyone can live a bright and happy life, just like Cotton Bread!

About the Book

Tired of the nightly struggle to get your child to sleep? Transform bedtime into a **magical experience with 16 Bedtime Stories for Kids Ages 4-8**.

Written by Cotton Bread, this enchanting collection brings a world of wonder, laughter, and valuable life lessons right to your child's pillow. Each story is thoughtfully crafted to spark imagination, calm restless minds, and make bedtime their favorite time of the day.

In this book, you will discover:

- **Adventures to Spark Creativity**: From talking animals to magical lands, every story is packed with excitement and wonder.
- **Life Lessons with a Gentle Touch**: Stories teach kindness, courage, and patience in a way kids love.
- **Perfectly Sized Tales**: Each story is just the right length for bedtime—enough to captivate, not overwhelm.
- **Relaxing and Soothing Themes**: Calm narratives to help kids drift into a peaceful sleep.

- **A Treasure Trove of Memories**: Create bonding moments as you and your child explore these delightful tales together.

From helping a shy dragon make friends to uncovering the magic of a kindness stone, every story is designed to entertain and inspire. Whether you're reading aloud or they're following along, these tales will keep young minds engaged and hearts warm.

Don't let another night of restless tossing and turning pass by. **Bring joy, peace, and unforgettable stories to your child's bedtime routine**. Scroll up and grab your copy today!

The Wishing Fountain

Sophia was a brave and kind 13-year-old girl who loved her family very much. But life at home had been sad for the past two years because her mom was very sick. Her mom couldn't walk or eat much, and she only drank milk to keep her strength. Every day, Sophia watched her mom grow thinner and weaker, and her heart ached to see her like this.

While helping her neighbors carry baskets one afternoon, she overheard an old woman say, "In the next village, there is a magical Wishing Fountain. They say it can grant any wish, but the price is steep."

Sophia's ears perked up. "What kind of price?" she asked, setting down a basket.

The old woman replied, "For every wish granted, the wisher will lose all their hair. It's said to test how much you truly want your wish."

Sophia's heart raced. Her mom's smile flashed in her mind. She didn't hesitate for long. That night, she packed a small bag and left a note on the table: I've gone to find a way to make Mom better. I'll be back soon. Love, Sophia.

The journey was hard. After three days and nights of walking, Sophia finally reached the magical fountain. It glimmered under the moonlight, as if made of stars.

Sophia stood before it, trembling. "What if it doesn't work?" she thought, but then she imagined her healthy and happy mom and found her courage.

She took a deep breath and said, "Please, Wishing Fountain! I want my mom to be healthy again! I want her to walk, to laugh, to smile!"

The fountain shimmered brighter, and a soft voice seemed to whisper, "Your wish will be granted, but are you ready to pay the price?"

Sophia nodded firmly. "Yes. I'm ready."

After making her wish, she sat beside the fountain and began to cry. As tears rolled down her cheeks, she whispered, "I just want her to be happy again. I miss her so much."

When she stood up to return home, she felt a tug at her hair. Small clumps began to fall as she walked, but she didn't stop. On the third day, as she reached the gate to her house, most of her hair was gone.

"Sophia? Is that you?" Her mom's voice called out. Sophia looked up in surprise. Her mom was standing in the yard, feeding the chickens. She looked strong and full of life.

"Mom!" Sophia dropped her bag and ran into her mom's arms.

Her mom held her tightly. "What happened, my sweet girl? Where have you been? And your hair—"

Sophia smiled through her tears. "It's a long story, Mom. But all that matters is you're better now."

They held each other close, both crying and laughing at the same time.

Teaching from the Story

Sophia's journey teaches us that true bravery comes from love and selflessness. She shows that sometimes we must sacrifice to bring happiness to the people we care about. It reminds us that even the smallest acts of kindness can create miracles.

The Sky Painter

Allen was a kind and brave boy who loved animals and cared deeply for the environment. Every day, he saw things that made him sad. Animals in his neighborhood were hurt or chased away, the river near his house was filled with trash, and the land around him was polluted.

"Why are people so mean to the earth and its creatures?" Allen would often ask himself.

When he saw someone bullying an animal, he would shout, "Stop that! Animals deserve kindness too!" If he spotted someone throwing trash on the ground, he'd run over and say, "Hey, don't litter! Let's keep the earth clean!"

But deep down, Allen wondered, Can one kid make a difference?

One evening, as he sat on the hill watching the sunset, something strange happened. The sky didn't glow with its usual orange, pink, and purple. Instead, it was dull and gray.

"Even the sky is losing its color," Allen whispered. His fists clenched. "I have to do something. I can't let the world lose its beauty!"

Allen remembered something his grandmother had told him before she passed away. She spoke of a magical town called "Huitan," where a mystical painter lived. This painter's brush could bring anything to life.

"I'll find the painter," Allen decided. "Maybe he can bring the sunset back to life!"

The Journey to Huitan

On Saturday morning, Allen packed a small bag with food, water, and a sketch of a colorful sunset he had drawn.

As he walked through the forest, he met a talking fox. "Where are you going, little one?" the fox asked, tilting its head.

"I'm looking for the Sky Painter," Allen replied.

The fox's eyes sparkled. "Follow me. I'll show you the shortcut."

After crossing streams, climbing hills, and dodging a mischievous raccoon who tried to steal his bag, Allen finally arrived in Huitan.

At the center of the town stood a small cottage with vibrant colors dripping down its walls. Inside, a kind-looking old man was painting a picture of a flower that instantly bloomed on his canvas.

"Excuse me, sir," Allen said nervously. "I need your help. The sky has lost its colors, and the sunset is fading. Can you paint it back?"

The painter looked at Allen with wonder. "Why do you care so much about the sunset?"

Allen's voice trembled but was firm. "Because the earth is our home, and it's beautiful. If we don't take care of it, we'll lose everything special about it."

The painter smiled. "Your love for the earth is inspiring. Let's paint the sky together."

A Sunset Restored

That evening, Allen and the painter stood on the hill. With each stroke of the brush, brilliant shades of orange, pink, and purple returned to the sky. The sunset glowed brighter than ever, and Allen felt his heart swell with joy.

"Thank you," Allen whispered to the painter.

The painter patted Allen's shoulder. "No, thank you, young one, for reminding me that even one person can make a difference."

Teaching from the Story

This story teaches us that caring for the world, even in small ways, can lead to big changes. When we love the earth and its creatures, others might follow our example. Never underestimate the power of a kind and determined heart!

The Pocket Dragon's Lesson

Nine-year-old John raced out of his classroom as the school bell rang, clutching his backpack. He was eager to head to the woods behind the school, where he often played with his extraordinary little friend—his pocket dragon.

This tiny dragon was no ordinary pet. Last year, on John's birthday, his dad had gifted him a glowing egg. One night, the egg hatched, revealing a miniature dragon with shimmering scales. From then on, John and the dragon became inseparable.

"Ready for some fun, buddy?" John whispered as he felt the dragon wiggle inside his pocket.

The dragon chirped, its tiny sparks lighting up his pocket. Together, they often played tricks on unsuspecting classmates. Today, John had snickered as his dragon left scorch marks on books and licked water onto skirts, making it look like an accident.

"Did you see her face?" John laughed as they reached the woods. "She thought her book was cursed!"

The dragon gave a little puff of smoke in agreement.

But before they could climb trees or pick fruit, a group of older boys emerged from the trees.

"Well, look who it is," sneered one of them. "Little John, all alone."

The bullies pushed John around, tugging at his hair and spinning him in circles until he felt dizzy. One boy smirked and said, "Let's hang him upside down from that branch!"

John's eyes filled with tears. "Help me, dragon!" he cried.

With a flash, the pocket dragon leaped from John's pocket, its eyes glowing fiercely. It let out a roar—small but mighty—and shot out a burst of flames. The flames whooshed through the air, so bright and hot that the bullies screamed and stumbled back.

"Run!" one of them yelled, scrambling to his feet. They all ran away, tripping over roots in their haste.

When the bullies were gone, the dragon returned to its gentle self, nuzzling John's cheek. John hugged his brave little friend tightly, tears streaming down his face.

"Being bullied is awful," John murmured. "I never realized how much it hurts. I shouldn't have tricked my classmates. I'm sorry, dragon. I'll be better from now on."

The dragon chirped softly as if it understood.

From that day on, John never played mean tricks again. Instead, he used his dragon's abilities to help others, like rescuing a stuck kite or cheering up a sad friend. He realized that kindness was the best kind of magic.

Teaching from the Story

This story teaches us the importance of empathy. When John felt the pain of being bullied, he understood how his classmates must have felt when he played tricks on them. It reminds us to treat others with kindness because our actions can have a big impact on their feelings.

The Talking Tree

On a warm afternoon, Amira, an easily distracted 8-year-old, was walking home from school. As usual, her thoughts wandered, and she didn't pay much attention to her surroundings.

Suddenly, she noticed something strange: a small park she had never seen before, even though she passed this way every day.

"That's odd," she murmured, stepping inside.

As she walked, a deep, creaky voice called out, "Amira, come closer…"

Startled, Amira spun around. "Who's there?" she asked, her voice trembling.

No one was in sight. Then, to her amazement, she saw a large old tree with a trunk so wide it looked like it had stood there for centuries. The bark shifted slightly, and the tree seemed to be… waving?

"Down here, child," the voice said again.

Amira's jaw dropped. "A… talking tree?"

"Yes," the tree replied with a chuckle. "Come, sit beneath my shade. I have a story to share."

Curiosity overpowered her fear, and Amira sat down.

The tree began, "Long ago, this forest was filled with animals and laughter. But one day, the forest started to wither because no one listened to the whispers of nature. The streams dried up, the leaves fell, and soon, silence took over. A brave little girl came along, willing to listen. She learned the forest's secrets and brought life back by simply paying attention. Listening is more powerful than you think, Amira."

Amira's eyes widened. "That's amazing. But… what does it have to do with me?"

The tree bent closer. "You often miss important things because you don't listen, do you?"

Amira blushed. "Well, maybe…"

"Come back tomorrow," the tree said kindly. "I'll tell you more stories. But only if you're ready to listen."

Over the next week, Amira visited the tree every day. She sat quietly, soaking in the tree's tales of magical forests, talking animals, and brave heroes. She found herself eager to hear every word.

One evening, her mother received a surprising call from Amira's teacher.

"Mrs. Khan," the teacher said, "Amira has changed. She's focused, participating in class, and answering questions. It's like she's a new student!"

When her mom asked Amira about it, she just smiled. "Sometimes, you learn the best things by listening, Mom."

Teaching from the Story

Amira learned the importance of listening. We discover the world around us, understand others, and grow as individuals by paying attention. Listening is not just about hearing words; it's about truly caring and learning.

Lia and the Cloud Cat

Lia sat all by herself on the swing in her backyard, her face as gloomy as a rainy day.

"I'm so bored," she sighed. "There's nothing fun to do anymore!"

As an only child, Lia often felt lonely. She would spend her days lying on the couch watching TV or aimlessly swinging back and forth. Her parents were busy and couldn't always keep her entertained.

One afternoon, as she kicked her feet lazily on the swing, a fluffy golden cat darted past her.

"Whoa, where did you come from?" Lia wondered aloud.

The cat didn't stop, so Lia jumped off the swing and chased after it. The cat led her through her yard, across a small patch of wildflowers, and into a hidden meadow by a sparkling stream.

Lia froze in amazement. The meadow was unlike anything she'd ever seen. The grass shimmered a vibrant green, and the stream sang a soft, tinkling tune.

The cat stopped, scooped up a handful of dirt with its paw, and flung it into the air. Lia gasped as the dirt transformed into colorful clouds, each one glowing like a sunset.

"Is this magic?" Lia whispered, her eyes wide.

The cat turned to her and meowed. Lia took it as an invitation.

She crouched down, grabbed some dirt, and tossed it into the air. Just like the cat, she created a swirl of bright, puffy clouds.

"Wow! This is incredible!" Lia laughed as she made cloud after cloud. Pink, blue, golden—each one was prettier than the last. She played for hours, creating her magical sky in the meadow.

As the sun began to set, the cat finally spoke.

"Lia," it said, its voice soft and gentle.

"Y-you can talk?" Lia stammered.

"Of course," the cat replied with a flick of its fluffy tail. "You've been bored because you haven't found something you love to do. Why not try finding a passion and focus on it every day?"

Lia thought about this as she walked back home, the cat padding alongside her. The next day, inspired by the colorful clouds, she picked up her long-forgotten art supplies and started drawing.

She drew the cat, the clouds, and the magical meadow. Her drawings became more beautiful with each passing day.

When her teacher announced an art contest at school, Lia decided to enter. The top five winners would have their work displayed in a special exhibit. Lia worked hard every afternoon, pouring her heart into her art.

Lia didn't feel lonely anymore. She had found something she loved, and every day felt meaningful and exciting.

Teaching from the Story

This story reminds us that finding something we love can make every day brighter. By trying new things and exploring our passions, we can discover talents and joys we didn't know we had. Even small steps can lead to big changes in how we see the world.

The Clockmaker's Apprentice

Benjamin sat by his grandfather's bedside, holding his frail hand. His grandfather smiled weakly and whispered, "My boy, I am growing old. Promise me you'll keep learning and working hard, even if I'm not around."

Tears streamed down Benjamin's face. "I don't want to lose you, Grandpa! There must be something I can do to save you."

The old man chuckled softly. "Oh, Benjamin, no one can fight against time."

That night, Benjamin fell asleep crying. His dreams were restless, suddenly, he wasn't sure if he was dreaming anymore. A small girl with golden curls appeared before him, glowing faintly in the moonlight.

"Do you truly wish to save your grandfather?" she asked.

Benjamin nodded fiercely. "More than anything!"

The girl leaned closer. "There's a magical clock hidden in my family's treasure room. If you fix it and turn your hands to the right time, you can go back and relive the moments you miss most. But it's broken."

Benjamin's eyes lit up with determination. "That's okay! My grandfather is a clockmaker. I've watched him repair clocks a thousand times—I'll figure it out."

The girl hesitated. "It won't be easy…"

"I'll try!" Benjamin insisted.

She led him to a magnificent treasure room filled with glittering items. At its center sat a dusty, ornate clock with shimmering golden gears. It was beautiful but lifeless. Benjamin carefully carried it back with him, and when he woke up, he found the clock in his arms.

For the next week, Benjamin poured all his energy into repairing the magical clock. He read every book on gears and springs, practiced on his grandfather's old clocks, and tried again and again.

On the seventh day, just as he was about to give up, a soft tick-tock broke the silence. The clock came alive!

Benjamin's heart raced as he turned the hands to 8 a.m., a moment before his grandfather became ill. Then, with trembling hands, he whispered the magical password the girl had taught him.

In an instant, he found himself standing in his grandfather's garden. The air was warm, the flowers were blooming, and there, watering the plants, was his grandfather—healthy and smiling.

"Grandpa!" Benjamin shouted, running to hug him tightly. "I missed you so much!"

The old man chuckled, surprised but happy. "Why, Benjamin, what's gotten into you?"

Teaching from the Story

This story teaches us that determination and effort can overcome great challenges. When we work hard for something important, we often find unexpected solutions. Treasure every moment with loved ones, as time is the most precious gift of all.

Clea the Brave Mermaid

Clea was a beautiful mermaid who loved nothing more than swimming through the vast ocean with her older sister, Marina. She adored diving deep into the water to watch the colorful coral sway and schools of fish dart around. When she grew tired, Clea would float on the surface, basking in the sun's warm rays, the cool breeze brushing her face. From there, she could gaze at the distant mountains and the tiny fishing boats bobbing on the horizon.

One afternoon, Clea and Marina swam hand-in-hand to the surface, as they often did. But today, the sky was unusual—dark and stormy. Moments later, strong winds howled, and waves crashed wildly against the fishing boats near the shore.

"Something's wrong," Marina said, her voice tinged with concern.

"Look!" Clea pointed to one of the small fishing boats being tossed about by the waves. A man's desperate shouts echoed across the sea, followed by the sound of a child crying.

Clea and Marina exchanged worried glances. "We have to help!" Clea said, already swimming toward the troubled boat.

The waves grew fiercer, but Clea and Marina didn't falter. They reached the boat and saw a fisherman clinging to the edge, struggling to hold on. A young boy was huddled inside, tears streaming down his face.

"Hold on tight!" Clea called out, her voice clear despite the roaring wind.

With all her strength, Clea helped Marina lift the fisherman onto her back. Then she turned to the boy. "It's okay. We'll get you to safety," she reassured him. The boy hesitated but eventually reached for Clea's hand.

The mermaid sisters swam against the crashing waves, carefully carrying the man and the boy to the shore. When they finally reached the sand, the fisherman and his son collapsed, exhausted but safe.

"Thank you," the boy said between sobs, his eyes wide with awe. "You saved us! You're… mermaids?"

Clea nodded with a gentle smile. "Yes, and we're glad you're safe."

The boy wiped his tears and gave her a shy grin. "Please come back tomorrow. We'll make you a delicious lunch to thank you!"

Clea giggled and looked at Marina, who nodded in agreement. "We'd love to," Clea said.

That night, as Clea rested under the starry ocean, she felt a deep sense of happiness. She had faced her fears and helped someone in need, and it felt incredible.

Teaching from the Story

Courage isn't about being fearless; it's about doing what's right, even when things seem scary. Clea and Marina's bravery shows us the importance of helping others, no matter how big the challenge. Kindness and compassion can turn stormy seas into calm harbors.

The Teddy Bear's Secret

Late one quiet evening, baby Philip was fussing again. "He's crying nonstop," Mom whispered, rocking the cradle. Dad sighed, running a hand through his hair.

They had tried everything—soothing songs, gentle pats, even taking turns holding him—but baby Philip just couldn't settle. His tiny hands flailed as if he were having a bad dream.

At 2 a.m., both parents, utterly exhausted, drifted off to sleep on the couch. The house was finally silent—except for the soft sniffles from the crib.

Suddenly, something extraordinary happened. Philip's teddy bear, which had always sat quietly by his side, wiggled ever so slightly. Its plush arm reached out and rested gently on Philip's shoulder. The teddy leaned close and whispered something only Philip could hear.

Instantly, the baby stopped crying. His tiny face relaxed, and soon he was peacefully snoozing, the corners of his lips curling into a sweet little smile.

The next morning, Mom and Dad were amazed. Philip was still sleeping soundly, his face glowing with happiness.

"Look at him," Mom said, nudging Dad. "It's like he had the best dreams ever!"

From that night on, Philip slept deeply every single night. As the years passed, he grew into a happy, lively three-year-old who never feared bedtime.

One day, Philip's cousin Ben came to visit. They shared a room for the night, but Ben was restless, tossing and turning in his little sleeping bag.

"I had a scary dream," Ben whimpered, rubbing his sleepy eyes.

Philip sat up and smiled. "Don't worry, I have just the thing." He reached for his trusty teddy bear and placed it beside Ben.

"Is this supposed to help?" Ben asked, doubtful.

"Just wait," Philip whispered.

The teddy bear's arm stretched gently, resting on Ben's shoulder. A soft glow seemed to surround it as it smiled its magical smile. Slowly but surely, Ben's tense face relaxed, and he drifted into a peaceful sleep, his smile mirroring the bear's.

Teaching from the Story

This story reminds us of the power of comfort and kindness. Sometimes, a small gesture or a trusted companion can ease fears and bring peace to even the most restless hearts. Always treasure the little things that make you feel safe, and never underestimate the magic of love.

The Night Circus

"Ravi, I can't sleep," whispered five-year-old Sophia as she tiptoed into her nine-year-old brother's room.

"What's wrong, Sophia?" Ravi asked, sitting up in his bed.

Sophia pouted. "At school today, Clara showed off her new toy. It's shiny and expensive, and I asked Mom if I could get one too. But she said no. She said I shouldn't compare myself to others, but it's not fair!"

Ravi thought for a moment. He didn't like seeing his little sister upset. "Okay, how about we go for a little adventure? Maybe the cool night air will cheer you up."

Sophia's face lit up, and she quickly slipped on her slippers. Hand in hand, the siblings quietly crept out of the house.

As they walked under the silver glow of the moon, Sophia asked, "Where are we going, Ravi?"

Ravi grinned. "Let's follow the moon and see where it takes us."

The siblings wandered through the quiet neighborhood until they spotted a strange glow in the distance. Music floated through the air, growing louder with every step.

"What is that?" Sophia asked, her eyes wide.

"I don't know, but let's check it out!" Ravi said, pulling her along.

When they arrived, they couldn't believe their eyes. A magical circus stood before them, shimmering under the starlit sky. Golden lights twinkled on striped tents, and the air was filled with the scent of sweet cotton candy and popcorn.

They rushed in to explore. There were sparkling carousels, a room filled with glowing toys, and even a Ferris wheel that seemed to touch the stars. Strangely, there were no other people, and everything was free to enjoy.

"Ravi! Look at this!" Sophia squealed, hugging a soft stuffed unicorn she had found.

Ravi laughed, holding up a toy airplane. "This place is amazing!"

The two played and laughed all night. By the time they returned home, they were tired but happy.

The next day, Ravi had an idea. "Sophia, why don't we bring some friends with us tonight? They'll love the circus too!"

Sophia clapped her hands. "Yes! Let's do it!"

That evening, Ravi and Sophia brought their closest friends to the circus. Together, they played, laughed, and shared stories. Sophia forgot all about Clara's toy. Instead, she felt happy surrounded by her brother and friends, knowing she didn't need fancy things to feel special.

Teaching from the Story

Happiness isn't about having the most toys or being like others. It's about sharing joyful moments with the people you care about. Learning to appreciate what you have and creating fun adventures can make life truly magical.

The Rainbow Ladder

Dona was not a troublemaker, but today he skipped school. His classmates had teased him again about how poor his family was. Feeling hurt, Dona wandered through the bustling market.

As he walked, he overheard an elderly woman say to a man, "Do you remember the stories from our childhood? They said there's a Rainbow Ladder in Shaba Village that leads to the sky where treasures await!"

The old man chuckled. "Nonsense! No one's ever found it. Probably just a myth."

Dona's ears perked up. Could the Rainbow Ladder be real?

That evening, when he returned home, his mother sat by the table, her face clouded with worry. "Your father is very sick," she said. "But we can't afford a doctor. Let's pray he gets better."

Dona clenched his fists. He made a silent promise to help his family. If the Rainbow Ladder existed, it could be their salvation.

After dinner, while his parents rested, Dona packed a small bag. A bottle of water and a slice of bread were all he could carry. He slipped out into the night, determined to find Shaba Village.

When he arrived, the village was quiet, lit only by the pale glow of the moon. He wandered through empty streets, whispering to himself, "Where could the ladder be?" Hours passed, and dark clouds gathered, turning the night even darker. Soon, rain began to pour.

Dona took shelter in an old wooden hut, shivering from the cold and feeling disheartened. "Maybe it's just a story," he thought. But as the rain stopped, he noticed a faint glow in the distance.

Stepping outside, he saw something incredible: a vivid rainbow arching through the night sky, glowing softly against the darkness. It seemed to end just beyond the hill. "It's real!" he gasped, running toward it.

The rainbow shimmered in the moonlight, and when Dona touched it, it felt solid. Carefully, he began to climb. Each step filled him with hope.

At the top, he found a magical land filled with gold and jewels, all glowing faintly under the stars. He stood in awe but reminded himself of why he was there. "I only need a little to help Papa," he said, picking up a few golden coins.

When Dona returned home, the coins paid for his father's treatment. His father recovered, and Dona used the remaining gold to help other children in need. Though life didn't magically become easy, Dona's heart was full, knowing he had made a difference.

Teaching from the Story

This tale reminds us that bravery and selflessness can lead to wonderful outcomes. Dona's willingness to risk everything for his family shows that love and determination can overcome even the toughest challenges. True happiness comes not from greed, but from helping those in need.

The Firefly Parade

It was an ordinary evening when Kiana, a bright-eyed girl with a curious spirit, grabbed her mysterious bag like she did every night. "What's in there, Kiana?" her friend asked one day.

Kiana simply smiled and said, "A special secret. You'll see someday."

After dinner, Kiana wandered into her backyard, opened the bag, and the yard lit up with tiny golden lights. Inside were fireflies, their soft glow dancing in the cool evening air. Her grandmother had given her the bag before passing away, saying, "Take care of these little ones. They'll help you when you need it most."

One chilly evening, as Kiana admired the twinkling fireflies, a small squirrel darted toward her. It tugged at her dress with its tiny paws.

"What is it, little one?" she asked, kneeling down. The squirrel chirped insistently and tugged harder, pointing toward the woods.

Curious, Kiana grabbed her bag of fireflies and followed the squirrel. They walked deeper into the forest, the air growing colder and darker with every step. "I don't think I should go any further," Kiana muttered.

But the squirrel didn't stop. It led her to a narrow, overgrown path. Suddenly, she heard voices—children's voices.

"They sound scared," Kiana whispered, quickening her pace. She came to a clearing where an old woman was comforting a group of frightened kids.

"We've been stuck in the dark for a week," the woman explained. "The moon and stars won't shine, and even our candles won't light."

Kiana's heart ached for them. She opened her bag, and the fireflies streamed out, their warm, golden glow lighting up the entire clearing. The children gasped in awe, and their fear melted into joy.

"Look!" one child shouted. "The whole village is glowing!"

Kiana followed the children outside. The fireflies danced through the streets, illuminating every corner of the dark village. The once gloomy night transformed into a magical scene, full of light and laughter.

Kiana smiled and whispered, "Thank you, Grandma. Your gift truly is special."

Teaching from the Story

The story teaches that small acts of kindness can light up the darkest times. Just as Kiana shared her fireflies to brighten the village, we can share what we have to help others. Often, the simplest things hold the greatest power to bring hope and joy.

The Snowflake Wizard

Deep in the snowy mountains lived the Snowflake Wizard. Every winter, she worked her magic to create the most beautiful snowflakes. These weren't just white flakes—they came in all shapes and colors, sparkling like tiny jewels in the sky.

People from far away would visit the village to see these magical snowflakes. They believed watching the colorful snowfall would bring good luck for the year ahead. The villagers kept the wizard's magic a secret, letting tourists think it was a natural wonder.

But this year, something went wrong. Winter had arrived, but no colorful snowflakes filled the sky. Tourists grew disappointed and left early, and the villagers worried about losing their only chance to make money for the year.

One evening, a group of villagers knocked on the Snowflake Wizard's door.

"Wizard, where are the magical snowflakes?" an old man asked.

"I've already sent them into the sky," the wizard said, frowning. "Something must be wrong!"

The Snowflake Wizard climbed to the top of the mountain to investigate. There, she saw a group of tiny fairies fluttering in the air, giggling as they played with her colorful snowflakes.

"You little fairies!" the wizard scolded. "Why are you taking my snowflakes?"

"They're so pretty, we couldn't resist!" said one fairy, twirling with a bright pink flake in her hand.

"But these snowflakes aren't just for fun," said the wizard sternly. "They bring happiness and hope to the villagers. Without them, the people suffer."

The fairies paused, looking at each other. "We didn't know…" said another fairy softly.

"You must return them," said the wizard. "And if you truly want to help, you can make the snowfall even more magical."

The fairies agreed, flying high into the sky. They released the stolen snowflakes and sprinkled extra fairy dust to make them shimmer even brighter. The night sky lit up with dazzling colors as the snowflakes fell gently to the ground.

In the village below, people cheered and danced in the snow. "It's even more beautiful than before!" a child exclaimed.

The Snowflake Wizard smiled from the mountaintop, watching as joy returned to her village.

Teaching from the Story

The story teaches that even small actions can have a big impact on others. It's important to think about how our choices affect those around us. We can create something magical when we work together and care for one another.

Gianna and the Echo of the Hills

Gianna was a little girl who loved to sing. She would sing loud and clear in her backyard every day.

The birds would listen to her songs, and sometimes they would fly around happily when she sang a happy song. Other times, when she felt sad, the birds would sit quietly, listening to her sad tune.

One day, Gianna's favorite doll was broken by a neighbor. It lost one of its arms, and Gianna was so sad. She ran to the hills behind her house and sang as loudly as she could, "Oh no, my dear doll is broken. What should I do?"

Suddenly, a soft voice answered, "Don't worry, Gianna. Tomorrow, your mommy will get you a new doll."

Gianna stopped and looked around. "Who said that?" she asked, but no one was there. The next morning, to her surprise, her mommy gave her a brand-new doll! "How did she know?" thought Gianna. "I never told her my doll was broken!"

Later that day, Gianna sat in her room playing with the new doll. She still couldn't understand what had happened. So, she sang again, "How did my mommy know about the broken doll?"

The voice returned, "Your voice has magic, Gianna. Your song can echo into the future and bring answers to your questions."

Gianna was amazed. She realized that whenever she sang, her voice could reach the future and give her answers. But she kept this secret to herself, not telling anyone about her magical voice.

One day, Gianna's family went to visit her sick grandpa. He was very ill, and the doctors didn't know how to help him. The doctors said there were no good doctors nearby, and everyone felt sad and worried.

Gianna sat by the pond outside and sang a sad song, "Grandpa is so sick, what should we do?"

Once again, the voice answered, "Don't worry, Gianna. Take your grandpa to Samsgrove City. There is a doctor named Dr. Philips. He is the best doctor for your grandpa."

Gianna quickly told her family. "There's a doctor in Samsgrove City! His name is Dr. Philips, and he can help Grandpa!"

At first, her family didn't believe her, but they decided to check. To their surprise, they found Dr. Philips and he was able to help Grandpa feel better. Grandpa got better, and everyone was so happy.

Teaching from the Story

Sometimes, when we feel unsure or worried, it helps to talk about it. Gianna learned that asking questions and thinking about answers can help us find the right path. No matter what, it's important to keep believing in the magic of hope and kindness.

The Kindness Stone

Aurora lived in a small town. The kids were always naughty, and the adults didn't help each other. Aurora didn't like it there. She often went to the river to be alone, away from all the noise.

One day, Aurora sat under a big tree by the river. She felt a little sad, so she rested near a stone. The stone was the size of a soccer ball, and it didn't look special. But something about it made Aurora feel curious. She sat quietly and looked at the river.

Suddenly, a little rabbit hopped by. It was so excited but tripped over some thorns and got stuck. Aurora quickly ran over and helped the rabbit. "There you go, little rabbit," she said. The rabbit hopped away happily.

When Aurora returned to her spot, she looked at the stone. It was glowing! It wasn't just a small light—it was glowing pink! "Wow!" Aurora said, surprised. "How did that happen?"

The next day, Aurora was walking in town when she saw a kitten stuck in a tree. It was meowing, looking scared. Aurora quickly climbed up and helped the kitten down. "You're safe now," she said, smiling.

Afterward, Aurora went back to the river. She sat by the stone again and saw that it was glowing even brighter! This time, it was glowing yellow. "Maybe it's because I helped the kitten," she thought.

Over the next few days, Aurora helped more people in town.

She helped an old lady carry groceries, picked flowers for a neighbor, and helped a boy find his toy. Every time she did something kind, the stone glowed in a new color—green, blue, and even purple!

Aurora told the people in the town about the stone. "I think the stone shines brighter when we do kind things," she said. "Let's all help each other."

The people in the town were excited. They started helping each other every day. They cleaned the streets, took care of animals, and helped neighbors. The town became a happy place, and the stone glowed brighter than ever.

Now, the town wasn't full of mischief and lies. It was full of kindness. Aurora wasn't sad anymore. She was happy to be in a town where everyone helped each other.

Teaching from the Story

This story teaches us that kindness makes the world better. When we help others, we make them happy and our community stronger. Aurora showed that small acts of kindness can bring magic to our lives.

The Kingdom of Dreamcatchers

Alice was a little girl who loved dreaming, but her dreams were not like other kids' dreams. Instead of fun adventures, Alice's dreams were often scary and made her feel tired when she woke up.

One day, Alice had a bad evening. She accidentally spilled her soup at dinner, and her mom got upset. "Alice, you must be more careful!" her mom said, frowning.

Alice felt sad and went to bed early, skipping the rest of her dinner.

That night, her dream was different. She was leading an army of shadowy soldiers, yelling commands. "Chase her! Don't let her go!" Alice shouted. In her dream, the soldiers were spraying her mom with colorful beams of light.

When Alice woke up the next morning, something strange happened. "Mom, what happened to your arms?" Alice asked, noticing small bruises on her mom.

Her mom looked surprised. "I don't know, Alice. Maybe I bumped into something, but I don't remember."

Alice started to wonder. Could her dreams affect the real world?

The next afternoon, on her way home from school, Alice saw something scary. A woman was holding a little boy's hand as they crossed the street. Suddenly, a man ran up, snatched her bag, and pushed her hard. The woman fell, and a car nearly hit her! The boy started crying loudly.

Alice ran to help the woman. "Are you okay?" she asked, helping her stand up. The woman nodded, her voice shaking. "Thank you, dear, but he got away."

Alice felt angry but helpless. She wished she could stop bad people like that man.

That night, as Alice lay in bed, she made a wish. "Tonight, I'll catch that bad man in my dream," she whispered.

In her dream, Alice was a queen with a glowing golden crown. She stood in a magical castle surrounded by starry skies. Her dream soldiers bowed before her.

"Find that bad man!" Alice commanded. "Bring back the woman's bag and make sure he never does this again!"

The soldiers flew through the night, glowing like shooting stars. They caught the bad man, tied him up with sparkling ropes, and delivered him to the dream police. Alice watched proudly as the bag was returned to its owner.

The next day, Alice went to the market with her mom. To her surprise, the woman she had helped the day before ran up to her.

"Thank you, sweet girl!" the woman said. "The police called me last night. They caught the bad man! But they said something strange—he had bruises, and no one knows why."

Alice smiled, her eyes twinkling. She knew exactly what had

happened but decided to keep it a secret. From that day on, Alice decided to use her dreams to help people and make the world a better place.

58

Teaching from the Story

This story teaches us that kindness and bravery can make a big difference. Even when you feel small, your actions can help others in ways you might not expect. Alice discovered that her dreams could change the world, and she chose to use them for good.

The Invisible Friend

Mika was a shy little girl. She didn't like talking to people and felt scared around strangers.

At school, she didn't have any friends. She ate breakfast alone and stood quietly in the corner while others played games.

One day during recess, Mika was standing in her usual corner, watching the other kids play. Suddenly, she heard a voice.

"Why don't you go play with them?"

Mika looked around but saw no one. Strangely, she wasn't scared. She answered softly, "I don't have any friends."

"Well, I can be your friend!" the invisible voice said cheerfully.

"Really?" Mika asked, her eyes wide with surprise.

"Of course! Let's talk," the voice replied.

From that day on, Mika had a secret invisible friend. Whenever she felt lonely, she would chat with her. They talked about Mika's favorite books, her drawings, and even the stars she loved to look at.

Over time, Mika began to feel happier. She smiled more often, and her teacher noticed.

"Mika, you've been so cheerful lately. That's wonderful!" her teacher said with a kind smile.

Mika was surprised but just nodded quietly.

One day, her invisible friend said, "Mika, I can't stay with you anymore."

"What? Why not?" Mika asked, her voice trembling.

"Because it's time for you to be brave and talk to real people," the voice said gently.

"But… I'm scared," Mika admitted, looking down.

"You can do it, Mika! You've already changed so much. Your classmates will like you. Trust yourself!"

The next day at recess, Mika was standing nearby, watching the kids play as usual. Suddenly, a ball rolled to her feet.

She picked it up and looked around nervously.

"Mika! Come play with us!" one of her classmates shouted.

Mika hesitated for a moment. Then, with a deep breath, she smiled and ran to join them.

Teaching from the Story

Sometimes, we need a little help to believe in ourselves. Mika's invisible friend gave her the courage to try, but the real magic came from within her. When we are brave and take small steps, we can discover that others are kind and ready to welcome us.

* * *

The End